MW00948901

This book belongs to:

_____

Digital art by Callaway Animation Studios under the direction of
David Kirk in collaboration with Nelvana Limited.

This book is based on the TV episode "Stumped," written by Michael Stokes, from the animated TV series
Miss Spider's Sunny Patch Friends on Nick Jr., a Nelvana Limited/Absolute Pictures Limited
co-production in association with Callaway Arts & Entertainment,
based on the Miss Spider books by David Kirk.

Nicholas Callaway, President and Publisher
John Lee, CEO
Cathy Ferrara, Managing Editor and Production Director
Toshiya Masuda, Art Director
Nelson Gomez, Director of Digital Services
Amy Cloud, Editor
Raphael Shea, Senior Designer
Krupa Jhaveri, Designer
Christina Pagano, Digital Artist
Dominique Genereux, Digital Artist

Special thanks to the Nelvana staff, including Doug Murphy, Scott Dyer, Tracy Ewing, Pam Lehn,
Tonya Lindo, Mark Picard, Jane Sobol, Luis Lopez, Eric Pentz, and John Cvecich.

Library of Congress Cataloging-in-Publication Data available upon request.

Distributed in the United States by Penguin Young Readers Group.

Callaway Arts & Entertainment, its Callaway logotype,
and Callaway & Kirk Company LLC are trademarks.

ISBN 978-0-448-45098-8

Visit Callaway Arts & Entertainment at www.callaway.com

10 9 8 7 6 5 4 3 2 1   09 10 11 12

First edition, March 2009

Printed in China

Stumped

David Kirk

CALLAWAY

NEW YORK

2009

The last berry of the season hung glistening from a high branch. *That will make the perfect head for my mushroom-hunt scarecrow,* thought Shimmer.

From across the garden,
Squirt spied the same berry.
"There's the perfect
soccerberry ball for our last
game," he laughed.

"It's mine!" shouted Shimmer.

"No, mine!" shouted Squirt.

As they struggled, the berry
sailed toward the ground.

Shimmer swooped down to snag the berry and flew away.

But when she crashed into a flower, Squirt caught the berry. He tried to hide in a log, but Shimmer flew after him. She barely avoided the sticky web he'd spun.

"So you like traps, do you?" she cried.

Soon Squirt spied the berry hidden in an empty nest.

"Not clever enough, Shimmer," he said. But as he touched the berry, Shimmer's scarecrow pounced! Squirt jumped back with a scream.

"Gotcha!" Shimmer laughed.

Meanwhile, the rest of the family was preparing for a mushroom picnic, when they heard shouting.

"Mine!" Shimmer yelled.

"No, mine!" Squirt hissed.

Rushing outside, Miss Spider lassoed the berry.

"No," she frowned. "Mine."

"Stop wagging your mandibles," Holley demanded, "and apologize right now!"

"Sorry your ugly scarecrow won't have a head," said Squirt.

"And *I'm* sorry that you're the world's worst berry thief!" Shimmer replied.

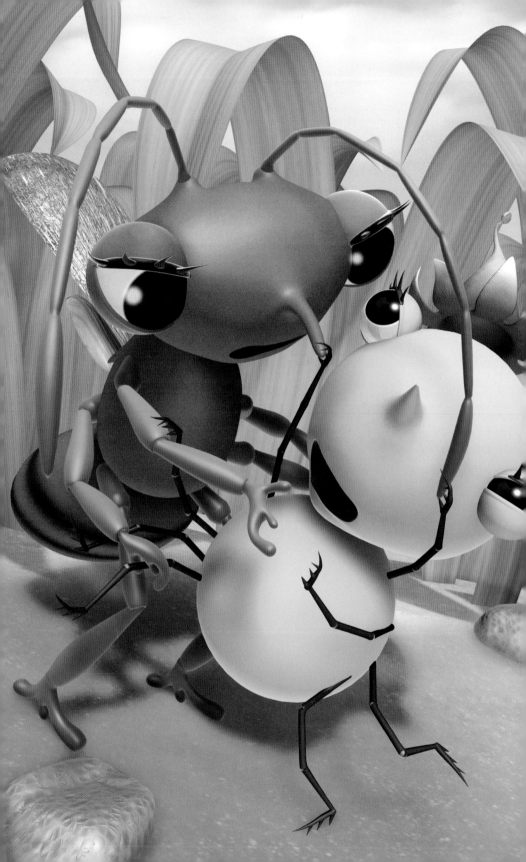

olley called for a handshake, but Squirt and Shimmer started arm wrestling instead.

Sighing, Holley admitted to Miss Spider that he was stumped.

"That's a great idea, Holley!" she exclaimed. "Stumped!"

Before they knew it, Squirt and Shimmer were sitting back to back on top of an old stump. "Neither of you will move until

each has forgiven the other,"
Miss Spider told them firmly.
The rest of the family left for
the picnic.

"It's *your* fault we're stumped," whined Shimmer. "I love mushrooms."

"I really wanted to go on that picnic, too," sighed Squirt. "But we don't have to just sit here."

Shimmer turned to see him spinning a trampoline web. He climbed aboard and *boing-boing-boinged* into the air. Shimmer joined him. Pretty soon they were performing some amazing flips.

Flopping down to catch their breath, the two bugs gazed at the sky.

"Doesn't that cloud look just like a flower?" asked Shimmer.

"No way!" said Squirt. "That looks like a frog."

They glared at each other, and then they started to laugh.

The bugs realized they were no longer mad at each other, and apologized for their mean words.

Squirt had an idea. "We should play a game of soccerberry and then use that berry as your scarecrow's head."

"It will look even scarier!" said Shimmer. "You've got a deal!"

They hopped off the stump just in time to see Grub pick up their berry.

"Lookee here," he said, taking a big bite. "I got the last berry of the season!"

Squirt and Shimmer burst into giggles.

"I thought I heard some little bugs laughing," said Miss Spider as she crawled over. "Are you two friends again?"

"Yep," Squirt and Shimmer chorused. "We're sorry."

"Then it's high time you joined the mushroom hunt," said their mother with a smile.

"Soon," Squirt said, pouncing on the trampoline.

"Yeah!" added Shimmer. "Right now we're having too much fun being stumped!"

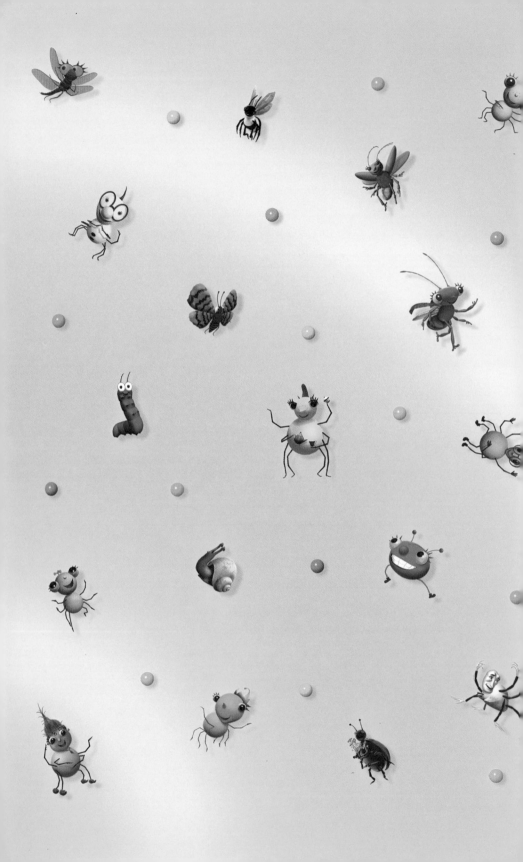